The Yellow Boat

DEAR CAREGIVER,

The books in this Beginning-to-Read collection may look somewhat familiar in that the original versions could have been a part of your own early reading experiences. These carefully written texts feature common sight words to provide your child multiple exposures to the words appearing most frequently in written text. These new versions have been updated and the engaging illustrations are highly appealing to a contemporary audience of young readers.

Begin by reading the story to your child, followed by letting him or her read familiar words and soon your child will be able to read the story independently. At each step of the way, be sure to praise your reader's efforts to build his or her confidence as an independent reader. Discuss the pictures and encourage your child to make connections between the story and his or her own life. At the end of the story, you will find reading activities and a word list that will help your child practice and strengthen beginning reading skills. These activities, along with the comprehension questions are aligned to current standards, so reading efforts at home will directly support the instructional goals in the classroom.

Above all, the most important part of the reading experience is to have fun and enjoy it!

Shannon Cannon

Shannon Cannon,
Literacy Consultant

Norwood House Press • www.norwoodhousepress.com
Beginning-to-Read™ is a registered trademark of Norwood House Press.
Illustration and cover design copyright ©2017 by Norwood House Press. All Rights Reserved.

Authorized adapted reprint from the U.S. English language edition, entitled The Yellow Boat by Margaret Hillert. Copyright © 2017 Pearson Education, Inc. or its affiliates. Reprinted with permission. All rights reserved. Pearson and The Yellow Boat are trademarks, in the US and/or other countries, of Pearson Education, Inc. or its affiliates. This publication is protected by copyright, and prior permission to re-use in any way in any format is required by both Norwood House Press and Pearson Education. This book is authorized in the United States for use in schools and public libraries.

Designer: Lindaanne Donohoe
Editorial Production: Lisa Walsh

LIBRARY OF CONGRESS CATALOGING-IN-PUBLICATION DATA
Names: Hillert, Margaret, author. | Baird, Roberta, 1963- illustrator.
Title: The yellow boat / by Margaret Hillert ; illustrated by Roberta Baird.
Description: Chicago, IL : Norwood House Press, [2016] | Series: A
 Beginning-to-Read book | Summary: "A yellow boat in a pond sails by its
 natural world including turtles, cattails, and ducks before being
 discovered by a young boy and taken to the boy's home"-- Provided by
 publisher.
Identifiers: LCCN 2016001864 (print) | LCCN 2016022136 (ebook) | ISBN
 9781599538112 (library edition : alk. paper) | ISBN 9781603579735 (eBook)
Subjects: | CYAC: Boats and boating--Fiction. | Toys--Fiction.
Classification: LCC PZ8.3.H554 Ye 2016 (print) | LCC PZ8.3.H554 (ebook) | DDC
 [E]--dc23
LC record available at https://lccn.loc.gov/2016001864

288N—072016
Manufactured in the United States of America in North Mankato, Minnesota.

Margaret Hillert's

The Yellow Boat

A Beginning-to-Read Book

Illustrated by Roberta Baird

Look here, look here.
See the little boat.
A little yellow boat.

The boat can go.
It can go away.
Go, little boat, go.

Away, away.
The boat can go away.

Oh, look, look.
Here is something.
It is funny.

Oh, my.
It can jump.
See it jump.
Jump, jump, jump.

Oh, oh, oh.
Something big is here.
Big, big, big.
Can it jump?

It can not jump.
It can go down, down, down.

Look here, look here.
One little one.
Two little ones.
Three little ones.

Where is the boat?
Where is it?
Find the little boat.

Oh, here it is.
Here is the yellow boat.

Go, boat, go.
Go away, away.

Here is something little.
It is blue.

It can go up.
Up, up, up and away.

Here is a mother.
Here is a baby.
A little yellow baby.

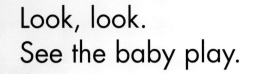

Look, look.
See the baby play.

And here is something.

Help, help.
Go away, go away.
You make me want to run.

Here comes something.
I see something little.

Oh my, oh my.
It is a little yellow boat.
See the yellow boat.

Oh, yellow boat.
I want you.
I want you.
Come to my house.

Here you go.
In here, in here.
Go, yellow boat, go.

Foundational Skills

In addition to reading the numerous high-frequency words in the text, this book also supports the development of foundational skills.

Phonological Awareness: The long /ō/ sound

Sound Substitution: Say the words on the left to your child. Ask your child to repeat the word, changing the short /o/ sound to a long /ō/ sound:

cot=coat	sock=soak	got=goat	slop=slope
rob=robe	hop=hope	mop=mope	rod=road
blot=bloat	clock=cloak	not=note	

Phonics: The long ō spelling

1. Make three columns on a blank sheet of paper and label each with these spellings for long /ō/: **ow, oa, oe**
2. Write the following words on separate index cards:

yellow	boat	rope	phone	coat
tote	float	road	slow	poke
home	grow	oak	quote	oats
blow	tow	goat	throw	note

3. Ask your child to read each word and place the card under the column heading that represents the long /ō/ spelling in the word.

Fluency: Shared Reading

1. Reread the story to your child at least two more times while your child tracks the print by running a finger under the words as they are read. Ask your child to read the words he or she knows with you.
2. Reread the story taking turns, alternating readers between sentences or pages.

Language

The concepts, illustrations, and text help children develop language both explicitly and implicitly.

Vocabulary: Sink or Float

1. Write the words sink and float on separate pieces of paper.

2. Provide your child with magazines that he or she can cut pictures from.
3. Work with your child to find images of objects that will sink or float. Help your child cut the pictures from the magazines and paste them on the correct piece of labeled paper.
4. Ask your child to name the objects and label them.
5. Ask your child to read the labels.
6. Notes:
   - You may choose to fill a tub of water and gather an assortment of objects to test whether they sink or float. You can ask your child to make a prediction before putting the objects in the tub of water and write the name of the objects on the correct labeled paper after the prediction is tested.

   - If magazines and/or objects are not available, write the following words on separate index cards and ask your child to draw pictures of each: rock, feather, string, stick, crayon, plastic spoon, metal spoon, paper clip, marble.

Reading Literature and Informational Text

To support comprehension, ask your child the following questions. The answers either come directly from the text or require inferences and discussion.

Key Ideas and Detail
- Ask your child to retell the sequence of events in the story.
- What baby animal did the yellow boat pass?

Craft and Structure
- Is this a book that tells a story or one that gives information? How do you know?
- Do you think the boy was happy to find the boat? Why do you think so?

Integration of Knowledge and Ideas
- If you could sail in a boat, where would you like to go?
- How do you think the boat got in the water in the first place?

WORD LIST

The Yellow Boat uses the 43 words listed below.

This list can be used to practice reading the words that appear in the text. You may wish to write the words on index cards and use them to help your child build automatic word recognition. Regular practice with these words will enhance your child's fluency in reading connected text.

a	help	not	up
and	here		
away	house	oh	want
		one(s)	where
baby	I		
big	in	play	yellow
blue	is		you
boat	it	run	
can	jump	see	
come(s)		something	
	little		
down	look	the	
		three	
find	make	to	
funny	me	two	
	Mother		
go	my		

ABOUT THE AUTHOR Margaret Hillert has helped millions of children all over the world learn to read independently. She was a first grade teacher for 34 years and during that time started writing books that her students could both gain confidence in reading and enjoy. She wrote well over 100 books for children just learning to read. As a child, she enjoyed writing poetry and continued her poetic writings as an adult for both children and adults.

Photograph by Glenna Washburn

ABOUT THE ILLUSTRATOR Roberta Baird is a freelance digital illustrator. She enjoys creating illustrations filled with rich details. Her work has been featured in magazines, books and in the educational market. Roberta currently resides in Texas with her husband, children and a wide variety of pets.